To:

From:

Date:

THE WEEKLY
Prayer Project
for Kids

JOURNAL, PRAY, REFLECT,
and **CONNECT** with **GOD**

WRITTEN BY MOLLY HODGIN

ZONDERKIDZ

The Weekly Prayer Project for Kids
Copyright © 2022 by Zondervan
Illustrations © 2022 by Zondervan

Requests for information should be addressed to:
Zonderkidz, 3900 Sparks Dr. SE, Grand Rapids, Michigan 49546

Library of Congress Cataloging-in-Publication Data

Names: Hodgin, Molly, author.
Title: The weekly prayer project for kids : journal, pray, reflect, and connect
    with God / Molly Hodgin.
Description: Grand Rapids : Zonderkidz, 2022. | Audience: Ages 8-12 | Summary:
    "The Weekly Prayer Project for Kids helps children 8 to 12 discover the
    power of all types of prayer and the impact it has in their lives. This year-
    long guided prayer journal encourages young readers to talk to God about
    their blessings, hopes, fears, and dreams, and more. Fun journaling prompts
    and beautiful photos and illustrations will keep kids engaged, while Bible
    verses and mindful reflections will deepen their faith as they begin their
    own personal relationship with God. And the weekly format is perfect for
    busy schedules while still building a regular habit"—Provided by publisher.
Identifiers: LCCN 2022003397 | ISBN 9780310141471 (hardcover)
Subjects: LCSH: Bible—Meditations—Juvenile literature. | Spiritual journals—
    Authorship—Juvenile literature. | Prayer—Christianity—Juvenile literature. |
    Children—Religious life—Juvenile literature.
Classification: LCC BS491.5 .H63 2022 | DDC 242/.5—dc23/eng/20220325
LC record available at https://lccn.loc.gov/2022003397

Art direction: Cindy Davis
Interior Design: Denise Froehlich
Illustrated by Kat Kalindi

Printed in China

22 23 24 25 26 / IMG / 10 9 8 7 6 5 4 3 2 1

Contents

Sadness and Grief

Intercession

Faith

Repentance

Awe

How to Use This Journal

Come and see what God has done,
his awesome deeds for mankind!

PSALM 66:5

The journal you hold in your hands isn't just a note-book or diary. It's not a school assignment you have to do for a grade. This is something much better—a place only for you, where you can learn more about God and yourself every week. A place where you can con-nect with God and learn to hear His voice more clearly when you pray.

Sometimes it can be tough to know the best way to talk to God and to hear Him talk to you, right? Luckily, God left us a guide in the Bible that shows us how to talk to Him through prayer, no matter where we are or what we're doing. There are seven types of prayers in the Bible. This book has a section for each type so you can try them all out. I promise that one of them will feel right when you want to talk to God.

Make this book your own! This journal was written for you, which means that the "right" way to use it is whatever you decide. Start at the beginning and work your way through, or jump ahead to the section that you want to explore in that moment. You can answer the questions inside with words or doodles or lists or whatever else you want to use!

At the end of the year, you can look back on your answers and see all the ways God has been there for you each week. And your answers will also remind you to keep talking to God in whatever way prayer feels right to you. I know He can't wait to hear from you!

Requests

Please, God

Take delight in the LORD, and he will give you the desires of your heart.

PSALM 37:4

If you ask your parents for things too often, they may get a little annoyed. So you pick and choose what to ask for and when to ask. If your dad is in a good mood, you might grab the chance to ask if your best friend can sleep over. If your mom is stressed with work and running behind, it might be the perfect time to ask her if you can order pizza for dinner. If your parents are grumpy, though, it might not be a great moment to ask for a new video game, right?

Luckily, God doesn't react the same way when we ask Him for things. We don't need to figure out if He's in a good mood or pick the right time to talk to Him when we ask for anything we need. It is always the right time to talk to God. He wants you to talk to Him. He wants you to ask Him for things. He wants to bless you.

Philippians 4:6 tells us to "pray about everything. He longs to hear your requests, so talk to God about your needs and be thankful for what has come" (VOICE). God wants to hear from you. He wants you to tell Him what you need and what you want. God happily hears, knows, and answers your prayers because He loves you.

Just ask.

WEEK 1
Ask Confidently

*Let us then approach God's throne of grace
with confidence, so that we may receive mercy
and find grace to help us in our time of need.*

Hebrews 4:16

Do you sometimes feel shy or scared to ask for help? That happens to everyone at some point. But you never need to feel shy or scared about talking to God. God has already promised to help you whenever you need Him. He's just waiting for you to ask!

In the space below, write down the things that you're usually a little scared to ask for, or the things that seem too small to bother God with.

God wants a close relationship with you, and He loves to answer prayers. List your prayer requests below.

WEEK 2

Don't Worry

Do not be anxious about anything, but in every situation, by prayer and petition, with thanksgiving, present your requests to God. And the peace of God, which transcends all understanding, will guard your hearts and your minds in Christ Jesus.

Philippians 4:6-7

Sometimes we worry about things that may happen in the future. *What if my best friend moves away? What if I fail my math test? What if? What if? What if?* Instead of freaking out, God wants you to bring those worries to Him. Tell God all of your what-ifs and ask Him to calm your mind and fill you with peace.

What are some of the what-ifs you are worrying about?

Take a moment to pray and tell God about all your worries. How do you feel now?

Nothing Is Impossible

Jesus looked at them and said, "With man this is impossible, but with God all things are possible."

Matthew 19:26

There are a lot of things that seem impossible, right? Like finding a hundred dollars on the street or getting to meet your favorite star. But God doesn't look at the world the same way we do. Nothing is impossible for Him. When you come up against the impossible, turn to God and ask for His help. He may just make the impossible possible.

Do you have any impossible (or just really difficult) things in your life right now? List them and then start asking God for His help.

_____

_____

_____

_____

_____

What are some big, awesome things God has already done in your life?

_____

_____

_____

_____

_____

_____

_____

_____

_____

_____

He's Listening

And if we know that he hears us—whatever we ask—we know that we have what we asked of him.

1 John 5:15

God is always listening—even in the middle of the night or very early in the morning. Even when you're in school or taking a walk or hanging out with your friends. If you talk to Him, He will always hear you. You never have to wonder if you are being too quiet or asking at the wrong time. Just start talking and know that God will catch every word.

Write down some of the things you want to pray about on the lines below. As you write, imagine your prayers going straight up to God.

When do you like to talk to God throughout the day, and why? And if you don't have specific times yet, which would work best to start?

WEEK 5

Have Cares

*Two blind men were sitting by the roadside, and
when they heard that Jesus was going by, they
shouted, "Lord, Son of David, have mercy on us!"
The crowd rebuked them and told them to be quiet,
but they cried out all the louder, "Lord, Son of David,
have mercy on us!" Jesus stopped and called them.
"What do you want me to do for you?" he asked.
"Lord," they answered, "we want our sight." Jesus
had compassion on them and touched their eyes.
Immediately they received their sight and followed him.*

Matthew 20:30-34

Two blind men asked Jesus for healing. They were
in pain. Jesus could have walked past them, but he
didn't. The Bible tells us that Jesus "had compassion"
and healed them. *Compassion* means that Jesus felt their
pain and wanted to help. Isn't that amazing? When you
hurt, God hurts with you. When you are suffering, God
is sad. When you are upset, God cares.

Is anything hurting you or making you sick right now? Ask God for healing on the lines below.

Think of a time when you felt sad or frustrated. Maybe you messed up or maybe something bad happened that you had no control over. How do you think God felt watching you go through that? What will you say to God the next time something like that happens?

Finding Forgiveness

Then he said, "Jesus, remember me when you come into your Kingdom." And Jesus replied, "I assure you, today you will be with me in paradise."

Luke 23:42-43 NLT

It's never too late to request something from God—in fact, Jesus died so that we could be forgiven and nothing could stand between us and God. In these verses, Jesus was on the cross. Next to Him, a criminal was also being punished. He asked Jesus for forgiveness. The criminal had spent his entire life sinning, and was within hours of dying, but it wasn't too late for him to ask Jesus for forgiveness. There is *always* time for you to ask for His forgiveness too.

Is there anything you can't seem to forgive yourself for? Have you talked to God about it?

Do you sometimes feel it's too late to ask God to forgive something you did, and so you just don't ask? Why do you think you feel this way? Can you ask for His forgiveness right now?

WEEK 7

Wait Expectantly

In the morning, LORD, you hear my voice;
in the morning I lay my requests before you
and wait expectantly.

Psalm 5:3

When we pray and ask God for something big or difficult or even a little challenging, it can sometimes feel like a long shot. We're praying, but we don't *really* think it will happen. Have you done that before?

But God doesn't want to be a long shot. He wants you to ask Him for anything and everything and *expect* Him to come through. He wants you to have faith that He is powerful enough to do the big and difficult and challenging, and that He will do those things *for you*.

Is there anything you've prayed for a lot, but never really thought would happen?

_____

_____

_____

_____

Waiting for big things to happen can be hard. Write down some things you waited for that eventually happened, and look at them whenever you need a reminder that God is always working to help you.

Thank You, God

*Consider it pure joy, my brothers and sisters,
whenever you face trials of many kinds,
because you know that the testing of your
faith produces perseverance. Let perseverance
finish its work so that you may be mature
and complete, not lacking anything.*

JAMES 1:2–4

Life can be tough sometimes. There are bad days, failed tests, teams you didn't make, and people who let you down.

We can choose to focus on all of the stuff that doesn't go our way, but that usually just makes us feel worse. Or we can choose to look for all of the ways God blesses us each and every day. For every thing we don't get, there are things we *do* get. For all of the tests we fail, there are many assignments we rock. For every situation that doesn't go our way, there are others that go exactly as we hoped.

We can be grateful, even on our worst days, because our hope and joy doesn't really depend on everything going right. Our hope and joy come from God, and He gives those things to us no matter what is happening in our lives. Isn't that wonderful?

When you pray, thank God for giving you everything you need and everything that matters. James 1:2–4 tells us to consider it "pure joy" when we go through hard things because we know that God uses those times for our good. So thank God for the good stuff *and* the bad stuff because you can have faith that God will turn that bad stuff into something good someday.

WEEK 8

Be Thankful

Enter into His gates with thanksgiving,
And into His courts with praise.
Be thankful to Him, and bless His name.

Psalm 100:4 NKJV

What does it mean to enter the Lord's gates with thanksgiving and His courts with praise? Well, every time you pray, it's like you are entering into God's home (past His gates and into His courts) to talk to Him. So start every prayer by thanking God for all of the good things He has done for you to make sure your heart starts in the right place. Talking about those things with God every day will also help you *really* notice all the good things to come.

What do you want to thank God for this week?

_____

_____

_____

_____

Below, list three things about God that you are thankful for:

_____

_____

_____

_____

_____

_____

_____

_____

_____

_____

_____

WEEK 9
Child of God

Jesus declared, "I thank you, Father, Lord of heaven and earth, that you have hidden these things from the wise and understanding and revealed them to little children; yes, Father, for such was your gracious will."

Matthew 11:25-26 ESV

In these verses, Jesus thanked God for revealing Himself to kids—that's you! God has gifted you with faith that grown-ups don't always have. Because you're young, you understand things that older people have forgotten—like that you don't have to do everything on your own and that it's okay to ask for help. God loves it when we ask Him for help, and He loves to hear our thankful prayers for all that He does for us.

Write about the day you invited Jesus into your heart. How did it feel? (And if you haven't done it yet and you feel ready, ask an adult to help you do it now.)

How can you thank Jesus for saving you?

Sacrifice of Praise

"But I, with shouts of grateful praise,
will sacrifice to you.
What I have vowed I will make good.
I will say, 'Salvation comes from the LORD.'"

Jonah 2:9

To understand just how big Jonah's prayer was in this verse, you have to remember *where* he was at the time. Jonah was praising God from inside the belly of a giant fish. A *fish*. Talk about having a bad day! But Jonah shows us that God is worthy of worship even during our most difficult times. Jonah didn't know what God's plan was or how being eaten by a giant fish was a part of that plan, but he trusted that God's plan was a good one. There will be times when you don't understand God's plan, but you can always trust that it's a good one and be thankful for His planning in your life.

Is there a reason you haven't been praising God in your prayers?

Circumstances change, but God doesn't. You can praise Him for who He is, even when life is tough. What can you praise God for this week?

WEEK 11
Not Shaken

Therefore, since we are receiving a kingdom that cannot be shaken, let us be thankful, and so worship God acceptably with reverence and awe, for our "God is a consuming fire."
Hebrews 12:28-29

You were created to live with God in heaven someday. Heaven is the kingdom that cannot be shaken. That means that once you let Jesus into your heart, no one can take heaven away from you. God loves us all so much that He promises we have a place in heaven, even though we mess up and make mistakes. Can you think of anything more amazing or worthy of our thanks than that? God's grace is something we can always be grateful for.

Does anything in your life feel shaky right now? Like it could be taken away or fall apart? Why do you think it feels like that?

We don't usually think about the promise of heaven in our everyday life. What do you think life might look like if we did? Would you do anything differently?

WEEK 12

Joy in Community

*We always thank God, the Father of our Lord
Jesus Christ, when we pray for you, because
we have heard of your faith in Christ Jesus
and of the love you have for all God's people.*

Colossians 1:3-4

In these verses, Paul and Timothy told their friends that they always thank God for their friendship because of their friends' faith in Jesus. Friends like that are awesome! We all need some friends we can share our faith with.

Do you have friends who love Jesus too? What's different or special for you about those friendships?

_____

_____

_____

_____

_____

Write God a thank-you note for your friends. Thank Him for the ways they help you to be your very best.

WEEK 13

Worship

Sing to the LORD with grateful praise;
make music to our God on the harp.

Psalm 147:7

Do you like music? God loves to hear our songs of joy and praise for all of the good stuff He's put in our lives—however you decide to celebrate Him. The next time you are feeling extra grateful to God, worship Him with music by singing, playing an instrument, dancing, or whatever feels right to you. He'll love it.

What is your favorite way to praise God in church?

Which things in your life inspire you thank God with worship whenever you see or hear them?

_____

_____

_____

_____

_____

_____

_____

WEEK 14
Rejoice Always

*Rejoice always, pray continually, give
thanks in all circumstances; for this is
God's will for you in Christ Jesus.*
1 Thessalonians 5:16-18

It's easy to praise God when things go right in your life. But it is a lot harder to thank Him when things go wrong, isn't it? If all of your happiness and joy in life depends on things going well all the time, you will be disappointed, because life will not always go your way. But if you get your joy and hope from your relationship with God, you can have sunny times on even the stormiest of days.

Think about the last bad day you had. Was it all bad? Or were there some good moments in there too?

Let's make a list of the things you can always be thankful for even on tough days. Add to this list as you think of more.

1. God loves me.

2. Jesus saved me.

3. God has a purpose for me.

4. ....

5. ....

6. ....

7. ....

8. ....

9. ....

10. ....

11. ....

12. ....

13. ....

14. ....

Sadness and Grief

Why, God?

"Never will I leave you; never will I forsake you."

HEBREWS 13:5

Sometimes life isn't fair. You can be the best kid—someone who always listens to your parents, reads your Bible, is kind to your siblings and friends, tells the truth, and does what's right—and bad things will still happen to you. Yes, even if you are careful and cautious and make good choices. There's no way to always avoid the stuff in life that hurts.

The Bible is filled with stories of people who struggled, people who were in pain, and people who were sad or angry or miserable. Stories of people who lost loved ones, whose homes were swept away by floods or burnt in fires, and who got sick. These things still happen all over the world. Maybe something like that has already happened to you. God never promises any of us will have an easy road in life. In fact, He has actually promised that we will all struggle (see John 15:20). But He also promises that we never have to struggle alone. When we have rough days, God is still good and He is still with us.

Jesus was human like us. He knows how it feels to struggle, to be in pain, to hurt, and to cry. He felt all of the pain of the cross *for* us. He can handle your pain too. When you pray to Him and tell Him about your struggles, He will be there to help you.

WEEK 15
Troubled Soul

May my prayer come before you;
turn your ear to my cry.
I am overwhelmed with troubles
and my life draws near to death.

Psalm 88:2-3

Sometimes life can feel like way too much: School becomes too difficult. Your parents seem too demanding. And your friendships get too confusing. When it everything becomes too much to deal with, that's the moment you know it's time to talk to God. Nothing is too much for Him. Tell God all about what you're going through—every last detail—and ask Him to help make it easier for you to handle. He will.

Have you ever had that "too much" feeling? When was it? What finally made it feel a little easier to deal with?

_____

_____

_____

_____

Does it sometimes feel silly to tell God about all of your problems? Why or why not?

_____

_____

_____

_____

_____

_____

WEEK 16
Run to God

For I am convinced that neither death nor life, neither angels nor demons, neither the present nor the future, nor any powers, neither height nor depth, nor anything else in all creation, will be able to separate us from the love of God that is in Christ Jesus our Lord.

Romans 8:38-39

Sometimes, pain can make God feel far away. When we are hurting or sick, all those big feelings we have can trick us into thinking that we have to face it alone. But those big feelings are wrong because nothing can separate us from God. He will always hear us, always be with us, and always love us. When you feel alone, pray; you will instantly feel closer to Him.

Have you ever felt like God was far away when you wanted Him close? What made you feel that way?

Do you have big feelings sometimes? What usually happens when you get those big feelings?

_____

_____

_____

_____

_____

Pray about your feelings right now—whether they're big or small, manageable or a little overwhelming. Did it make a difference?

_____

_____

_____

_____

_____

_____

Turn to Joy

"Very truly I tell you, you will weep and mourn while the world rejoices. You will grieve, but your grief will turn to joy."

John 16:20

As Christians, we have so much reason for hope. Yes, we will have pain and sadness, just like anyone else, but we also *always* have Jesus. He has promised to turn our sadness and pain into joy. He doesn't promise us exactly how or when He will do that, so keep your eyes open for joy, even when things are tough. It will come.

Describe a time you found joy when things were tough for you.

_____

_____

_____

_____

_____

Write down things that bring you joy when you are sad or struggling. Can you do one of those things today?

WEEK 18

Meets Needs

*And my God will meet all your needs according
to the riches of his glory in Christ Jesus.*

Philippians 4:19

Sometimes we ask God for things we want or think we need, and He says no. That can feel really frustrating. After all, we know that God can do *anything,* so why won't He do this one little thing for us? The truth is, God gives us what we actually need most, not what we really want or what we think we need. He sees the big picture that is hidden from us and He knows what is best for us, even if we can't see it yet. Trust Him, *especially* when He says no. He always has a reason.

What have you asked for that God has said no to?
Do you think it was a "no" or a "not yet"?

Write a thank-you prayer for God here that you can use the next time He tells you no. When you feel frustrated or let down, this will help you remember that God says no because it's what's best for you.

WEEK 19
Too Heavy

Praise be to the Lord, to God our Savior,
who daily bears our burdens.
Psalm 68:19

Pain and sadness and difficult times can feel very heavy. Big feelings and stress use up a lot of energy and leave us feeling worn out. You can't ask your mom or your brother or your best friend to help you carry your feelings, but you can ask God. He will calm your emotions, soothe your stress, and make your problems feel lighter.

Tell God what you're carrying that feels too heavy.

Now ask God to help make it lighter for you. How does that feel?

God Answers

I call on the LORD in my distress,
and he answers me.

Psalm 120:1

God promises that He will answer our prayers. He never promises He will always say yes or that He will answer them the way we might want him to, but He does promise to answer. So you can pray confidently. You can trust that even if He doesn't "fix" your problems the way you hope they will be fixed, He hears your prayers and answers in His perfect way. And God's way is perfect.

Has God ever fixed a situation for you, just not in the way you wanted Him to? How did that work out?

Do you immediately turn to God when things are tough, or do you first try to fix it all yourself? How does that usually go?

_____

_____

_____

_____

_____

_____

_____

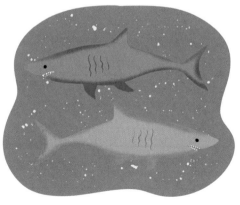

Supernatural Comfort

Blessed are those who mourn,
for they will be comforted.

Matthew 5:4

God has promised to comfort you when you hurt. This is true for little things as well as much bigger things. God sees all of your hurts and He perfectly understands what you are going through, so talk to Him about it all and let Him comfort you.

Have you ever felt hurt by someone or something? What made you feel better?

Do you know anyone who is hurting right now?
What are some things you could do to comfort
them?

Intercession

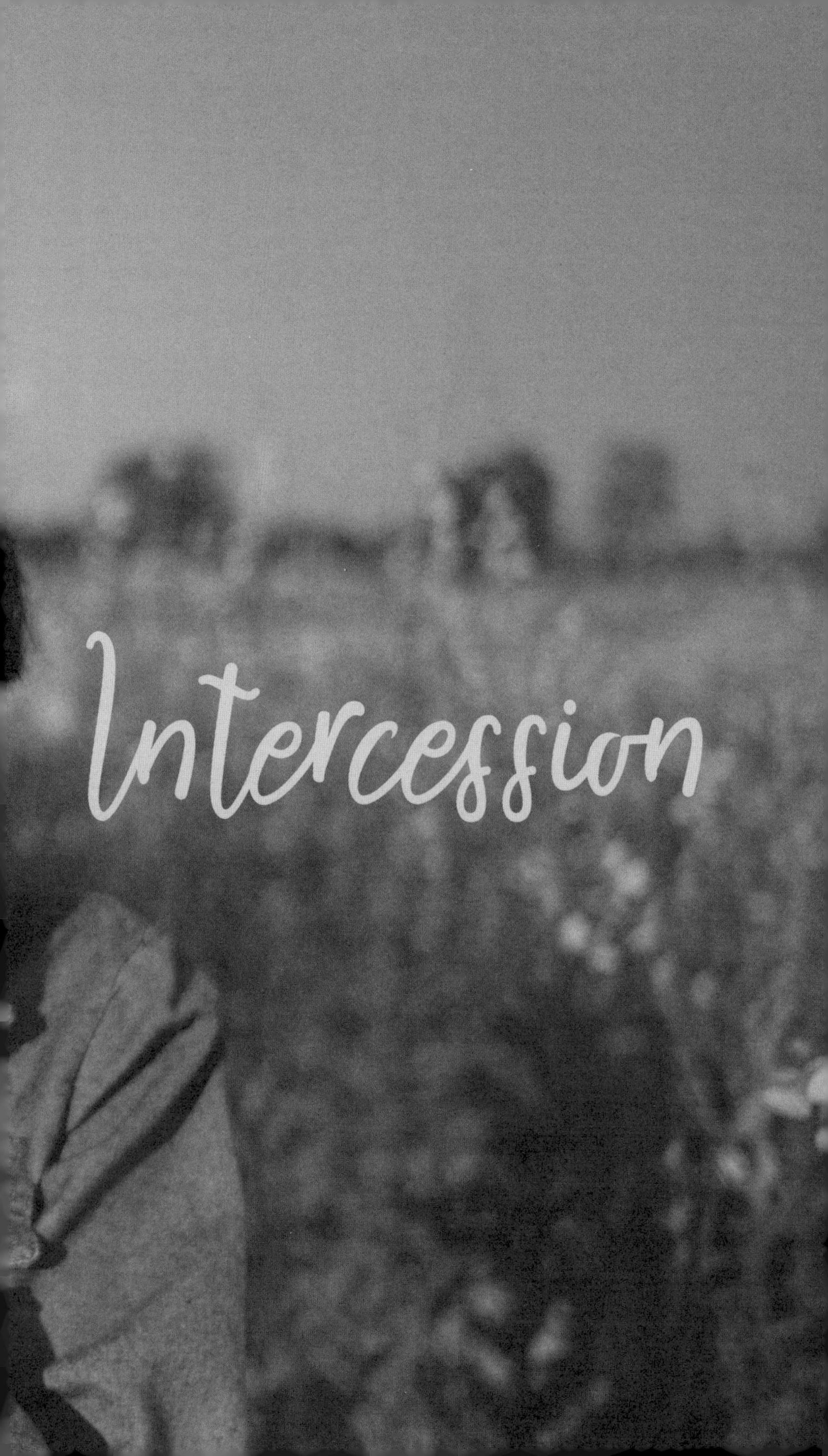

Help, God

*And pray in the Spirit on all occasions
with all kinds of prayers and requests.
With this in mind, be alert and always
keep on praying for all the Lord's people.*

EPHESIANS 6:18

Intercession is an action prayer. It means to pray for help for someone. When we pray to ask God to step in, to help us, to protect us, or to be with us, we are asking Him to intercede (or act) for us. We are praying a prayer of intercession.

God intercedes all the time in the Bible. When He parted the Red Sea for Moses, He interceded to save the Israelites. God interceded when He brought down the walls of Jericho through Joshua. And Jesus interceded when He died on the cross so that we could be forgiven.

God intercedes for you even today. When you ask Him for help for yourself or for someone else and He comes through, that's intercession at work. Prayers of intercession are powerful.

As children of God, we can also intercede for others with our prayers. You can pray for your brother when he's lying to your parents. Or pray for that kid on your soccer team whose dad is always yelling at him. Or for your friend who doesn't know Jesus yet. James 5:16 tells us that our prayers have great power. You can pray and ask God for healing, protection, and love for everyone around you. He'll listen.

No Words

We are very weak, but the Spirit helps us with our weakness. We do not know how to pray as we should. But the Spirit himself speaks to God for us, even begs God for us. The Spirit speaks to God with deep feelings that words cannot explain.

Romans 8:26 ICB

The Holy Spirit is the day-to-day connection between you and God. Often, the Holy Spirit knows what's in your heart and what you need even better than you do. When you feel lost or confused or you don't know *what* to say to God, let the Holy Spirit help you out. As you start praying, ask the Holy Spirit to speak for you. Then be still and see what happens.

Do you ever struggle to talk to God? Do you worry you've been saying the wrong things?

_____

_____

_____

_____

Practice letting the Holy Spirit speak for you when you pray. Do you think God understood you?

Burden Bearer

Carry each other's burdens, and in this
way you will fulfill the law of Christ.

Galatians 6:2

No one ever goes through life alone—even when it may not feel like it, there is always someone thinking about and caring for you. Jesus taught us to be there for each other and help other people. As Christians, we need to pray for the Holy Spirit to help us notice when others need us. Then, we will have the chance to intercede and help others the same way that God helps us.

How have other people supported you during tough times? How did their help show you more of God's love?

Does someone in your life need help? How can you help this person?

When People Pray

The men turned away and went toward Sodom,
but Abraham remained standing before the LORD.
Then Abraham approached him and said: "Will
you sweep away the righteous with the wicked?"
[...] Then he said, "May the Lord not be angry, but
let me speak just once more. What if only ten can
be found there?" [God] answered, "For the sake of
ten, I will not destroy it."

Genesis 18:22-23.32

Abraham begged God to save all of the people in a wicked city if ten good people could be found there, and God said yes. This is one of many examples of God acting when people pray for others.

Write down the names of three people you want to pray for and their specific situations. How would you like to see God work in their lives?

_____

_____

_____

Commit to praying for these people every day this week. Then, if you see God answer that prayer, write down how He answered and put the date beside it.

Spiritual Wisdom

I have not stopped giving thanks for you, remembering you in my prayers. I keep asking that the God of our Lord Jesus Christ, the glorious Father, may give you the Spirit of wisdom and revelation, so that you may know him better.

Ephesians 1:16-17

In these verses, Paul gave us an example of how to pray for others. He prayed that the Ephesians would come to know God better. We can pray for a lot of things for the people in our lives, but wanting them to know God better should be at the top of the list.

Is there anyone in your life you'd like to intercede for, so they get to know God better? Why?

Would you like to know God better yourself? What can you do to grow closer to Him (other than praying, of course!)?

WEEK 26
Praying Sacrificially

So Moses returned to the LORD and said, "Oh,
what a terrible sin these people have committed.
They have made gods of gold for themselves. But
now, if you will only forgive their sin—but if not,
erase my name from the record you have written!"

Exodus 32:31-32 NLT

Moses cared deeply for the Israelites. When he found them worshiping a golden calf they had made, he interceded for them with God. Moses asked God to forgive the sins of His people, even if it meant sacrificing himself. Can you think of someone who did that for all people? Yep, Jesus.

Have you ever sacrificed something you wanted in
order to help someone? What happened?

_____

_____

_____

_____

How did sacrificing for someone make you feel?

Let Love Abound

And this is my prayer: that your love may abound more and more in knowledge and depth of insight, so that you may be able to discern what is best and may be pure and blameless for the day of Christ, filled with the fruit of righteousness that comes through Jesus Christ—to the glory and praise of God.

Philippians 1:9–11

Paul prayed that the people at the church in Philippi would be "filled with the fruit of righteousness" that comes from Jesus. "Fruit of righteousness" is fancy way of saying good qualities that come naturally when we invite Jesus into our hearts. Qualities like unconditional love, joy, peace, patience, kindheartedness, goodness, faithfulness, gentleness, and self-control. Paul interceded for his friends, praying they'd receive blessings from God. We can intercede in the same way for our friends.

What do you think being "filled with the fruit of righteousness" looks like in action? See Galatians 5:22–23 for some ideas.

Is there a friend in your life you would like to intercede for with God? Write out the blessings you'll ask for here.

Confess and Pray

Confess your sins to one another and pray for one another, that you may be healed. The prayer of a righteous person has great power as it is working.

James 5:16 ESV

Our first instinct when we do something wrong is to cover it up so that no one else finds out. But that is never actually a good plan. Carrying around the mistakes you've made (and the bad feelings that come along with those mistakes) just makes you feel worse. Admitting when you've done something wrong and asking for forgiveness is the only way to heal those bad feelings. When we share our mistakes with friends and ask them to pray for us, their intercession can help us let go of those bad feelings and feel closer to God again.

Do you have friends or family you can admit your mistakes to and ask for help?

Do you pray for those people? Do they pray for you? If not, have you asked them to pray for you?

Are You Sure, God?

"Truly I tell you, if you have faith as small as a mustard seed, you can say to this mountain, 'Move from here to there,' and it will move. Nothing will be impossible for you."

MATTHEW 17:20

The world is filled with things that we won't ever fully understand or be able to control. Things like why some people get sick while others stay healthy or why some people have everything they need and others struggle to get by each day. Luckily, we don't have to be in control, because God is always in complete control, and we have faith in Him.

Having faith means that we trust and believe in who God is and what He can do. But sometimes it can be difficult to have faith, can't it? After all, you've never seen God. You've never felt Him give you a hug or wipe away your tears. You haven't heard Him tell you a story or sing a song with you. And yet, you are reading this book because you *know* He is there, even if you can't see or touch or hear Him. You know He's there because you have faith.

Faith can move mountains. When we pray with faith, believing that God can answer, He will answer. We have a loving, mighty Father in heaven who loves to show us what He can do when we believe.

Trust God

*Trust in the LORD with all your heart
and lean not on your own understanding;
in all your ways submit to him,
and he will make your paths straight.*

Proverbs 3:5-6

God isn't just there to talk to when you have a problem or need advice. He should be the One you tell *everything* to *every day*. Sure, you should talk to your parents, teachers, and trusted friends too, but none of them can make your path straight. God can be trusted absolutely and He, and He alone, knows the big picture for your life. When you talk to Him about everything you have going on, you can be sure you will keep moving in the right direction.

Do you only talk to God about big decisions or do you talk to Him about everything? Why?

Are you on a path that doesn't feel straight right now? Why? Ask God to help. Then come back to this page and write down how things have changed.

Struggling with Doubt

[Jesus] said to Thomas, "Put your finger here; see my hands. Reach out your hand and put it into my side. Stop doubting and believe." Thomas said to him, "My Lord and my God!" Then Jesus told him, "Because you have seen me, you have believed; blessed are those who have not seen and yet have believed."

John 20:27-29

Doubting Thomas earned his nickname because he struggled to have faith. In this passage, Thomas just couldn't believe that Jesus had been resurrected from the dead. Thomas wanted to see Jesus face-to-face and feel Him in the flesh to make sure. But God tells us that we are blessed because we have faith without ever being able to see or touch Him. That's a powerful thing.

Do you sometimes have doubts about God? Why?

How do you feel when you doubt God? Does anything make those doubts fade and strengthen your faith?

He Listens

Because he turned his ear to me,
I will call on him as long as I live.

Psalm 116:2

God isn't too busy for you. He isn't distracted by anything else when you talk to Him. He actively bends down to hear your prayers because He loves you so much. Isn't it comforting to know that God is always there? That you can always trust Him to listen? The more you trust God, the more your faith will grow.

How does this verse change how you think about prayer?

How can you be a better listener for the people in your life this week?

Impossible Prayers

"Truly I tell you, if anyone says to this mountain,
'Go, throw yourself into the sea,' and does not
doubt in their heart but believes that what they
say will happen, it will be done for them. Therefore
I tell you, whatever you ask for in prayer, believe
that you have received it, and it will be yours."

Mark 11:23-24

God answers prayers. He did it for the first people He created, and He still does it today. He answers prayers about small things, big things, and seemingly impossible things. But big prayers require big faith. When you pray to Him with faith, fully trusting that He will answer you, God can and will do big things for you.

Have you ever prayed for anything big or seemingly impossible? What was it?

Write out a list of big things you can pray for today. Which do you want most? Pray and ask God for it, doing your best to believe God will answer in a big way.

1. ....

2. ....

3. ....

4. ....

5. ....

6. ....

7. ....

8. ....

9. ....

Ask in Faith

If any of you lacks wisdom, you should ask God, who gives generously to all without finding fault, and it will be given to you. But when you ask, you must believe and not doubt, because the one who doubts is like a wave of the sea, blown and tossed by the wind.

James 1:5-6

Having wisdom is different than being smart. If you are smart, you learn things quickly and easily. If you have wisdom, you make good choices for yourself and others. James 1:6 urges you to ask in faith for wisdom, without doubting you'll receive that wisdom. It can be tough to admit that you aren't wise and ask for help, but we all need more of God's wisdom. He wants you to believe Him. And He wants your prayers to reflect that.

In what ways are you smart? In what ways are you wise?

_____

_____

_____

_____

_____

List the situations in your life where you want to be wise. Pray, believing that God will help you.

1. _____

2. _____

3. _____

4. _____

5. _____

6. _____

7. _____

8. _____

Pour Out Your Heart

Trust in him at all times, you people;
pour out your hearts to him,
for God is our refuge.

Psalm 62:8

Trust in God at *all* times. Not just sometimes. Not just when life is good, and your friends like you and you have straight As on your report card. Trust Him on the rough days when it looks like everything's falling apart, you feel alone, and you are failing. Because He's still there beside you. He is always there beside you.

What is a refuge? (Look it up in the dictionary if you need to!) How is God a refuge to you?

When do you feel you need to trust God the most?

Righteous Faith

What does Scripture say? "Abraham believed God, and it was credited to him as righteousness."

Romans 4:3

God saw Abraham as righteous. That doesn't mean that Abraham was a perfect man. In fact, the Bible talks a lot about Abraham's many sins. So how did God see a sinful man as righteous? Because Abraham believed with all his heart that God is who He says He is. We all sin. But we can also all have faith.

Which Bible story reminds you most of your own faith? Why?

_____

_____

_____

_____

_____

_____

Think about the Christians in your life. Whose faith do you admire, and why?

Help My Unbelief

Immediately the boy's father exclaimed, "I do believe; help me overcome my unbelief!"
Mark 9:24

This prayer is so honest. Are you ever afraid to tell God that your faith is weak? Do you ever pray, thinking, *This isn't really doing anything, but I know I'm supposed to do it?* Do you ever feel more alone when you're at church than you do when you are actually alone? That's okay. No one is perfect and everyone doubts sometimes. Luckily, God can take the tiniest seed of faith and help it grow into something big and beautiful. Pray now and ask God to strengthen your faith.

Do you think your faith is strong or weak? Why?

_____

_____

_____

_____

_____

Is there an area where your faith could be stronger?
How could you ask God to help you with this?

Repentance

I'm Sorry, God

*Repent, then, and turn to God, so that
your sins may be wiped out, that times
of refreshing may come from the Lord.*

ACTS 3:19

Have you ever forgiven someone with your words, but not with your heart? You say everything is fine, but you still feel angry and hurt?

You've likely been on the other side of that too. You apologized, and the person you hurt said they were okay, but things haven't been the same between you since then.

Luckily, God doesn't forgive that way.

When we were so wrong, so guilty, so hurtful toward God, He reached down from heaven and offered us forgiveness in Jesus. But not like the fake, holding-it-over-your-head-until-the-end-of-time examples in our lives. Jesus takes our sin and removes it from us "as far as the east is from the west" (Psalm 103:12 ESV).

All He asks for is repentance. Repentance is more than just apologizing. It means that you admit you were wrong, feel genuinely sorry for what you've done, ask for forgiveness, and work hard not to make the same mistake again. God wants each of us to come to Him with a humble heart that genuinely says, "I've wronged you. I need you. Please forgive me."

Ask the Lord to forgive you and find healing in his mercy.

Gracious to Forgive

And forgive us our debts,
as we also have forgiven our debtors.

Matthew 6:12

This verse is part of the Lord's Prayer—Jesus's example of how to pray. In this simple prayer of repentance, we ask God to make us as quick to forgive others as He is to forgive us. When we don't forgive others and instead hold on to our angry feelings, those feelings can make it harder for us to connect with God. God doesn't want you to walk around with an angry heart. Forgiveness turns that anger into love for those who hurt us, which helps you grow closer to Him.

Is there something you need to ask God's forgiveness for? Write out what you would like to tell Him.

Are you quick to forgive others, or does it take you a little while to be ready to forgive? Why do you think that is?

WEEK 38
Please Forgive Me

"You said, 'Listen now, and I will speak;
I will question you,
and you shall answer me.'
My ears had heard of you
but now my eyes have seen you.
Therefore I despise myself
and repent in dust and ashes."

Job 42:4-6

In Job 42, Job owned up to his sins and asked God to forgive what he had done wrong. What convinced Job to repent? He saw God's holiness (how He is greater than anything else, loving, and perfect), and it showed him just how much he had sinned.

Job couldn't see his own sin until he saw God's holiness. Think about God. Does it help you see your sins more clearly?

_____

_____

_____

_____

_____

When we repent, God blesses us. Below, write about a time you repented and saw God's blessing as a result.

_____

_____

_____

_____

_____

_____

No Regrets

*Godly sorrow brings repentance that
leads to salvation and leaves no regret,
but worldly sorrow brings death.*

2 Corinthians 7:10

As a follower of Jesus, your sins *should* cause you sadness and regret, making you want to repent. That is godly sorrow. When you know God, you can more clearly see how your mistakes and poor choices hurt others and hurt God. You feel badly about your actions, are genuinely sorry, and do your best not to make the same mistake again. Sometimes, however, you only regret your actions because you got in trouble. This is worldly sorrow. It doesn't make you want to repent or do better. When you've messed up, you know the difference. God does too.

When you mess up, what does it look like when you have godly sorrow?

What does it look like when you have worldly sorrow?

WEEK 40

Washed Clean

Have mercy on me, O God,
according to your unfailing love;
according to your great compassion
blot out my transgressions.
Wash away all my iniquity
and cleanse me from my sin.

Psalm 51:1-2

If you aren't sure how to repent, the Bible is full of examples. In this psalm, David prayed for God's forgiveness. He also talked about God's mercy, His love, and His compassion. David apologized for what he had done and asked the Lord to remove his guilt.

Why do you think David praised God while asking for forgiveness?

Why do you think David compared being forgiven to being washed clean?

WEEK 41
Return and Rest

This is what the Sovereign LORD,
the Holy One of Israel, says:
"In repentance and rest is your salvation,
in quietness and trust is your strength."

Isaiah 30:15

It can feel scary to come to God when we've messed up. Sometimes we try to hide or handle our mistakes ourselves. But when we come to God and repent, we find Jesus waiting with forgiveness and salvation. And when we stop worrying and trust God, we find His strength waiting to carry us through.

Do you think it takes more strength to be quiet and trust God to handle a situation or more strength to try to handle it yourself? Why?

What do you think it means to repent and rest in God?

Promise Keeper

*The Lord is not slow in keeping his promise,
as some understand slowness. Instead he
is patient with you, not wanting anyone to
perish, but everyone to come to repentance.*

2 Peter 3:9

When you sin, it creates a barrier between you and God. But when you repent, the barrier crumbles, clearing the way between your heart and God so you can draw close to Him. And God wants you to be close to Him so He can take away your guilty feelings and fill you with His promise of joy and peace.

What does it feel like when you pray and repent?

God keeps His promises, including His promise to forgive us when we repent. What other things does God promise us? (Hint: Search Scripture if you aren't sure!)

Forgive My Guilt

David was conscience-stricken after he had counted the fighting men, and he said to the Lord, "I have sinned greatly in what I have done. Now, Lord, I beg you, take away the guilt of your servant. I have done a very foolish thing."

2 Samuel 24:10

When you do something wrong, you always eventually feel bad for doing it. That's guilt. Guilt doesn't just go away on its own. If it isn't dealt with, guilt will make you sad and angry at yourself. To get past the guilt, you have to ask God for His forgiveness and also be willing to forgive yourself for messing up. We all mess up. But if God can forgive you, doesn't it make sense that you should forgive yourself too?

Do you feel guilty about anything right now?

Pray, asking God to forgive you and take away your guilt. How do you feel after talking with Him?

Repentant Hearts

Produce fruit in keeping with repentance.
Matthew 3:8

In this verse, John the Baptist was talking to the Pharisees, a group of religious people who thought they could get to heaven by following God's Old Testament rules perfectly. But they became so focused on following the rules that they forgot *why* the rules were there. God created His rules to keep our hearts repentant and focused on Him. If we follow the rules, but don't follow God, we've missed the point.

Would you say you are a rule follower or a rule breaker? Why?

_____

_____

_____

_____

_____

Do you know why you follow the rules you do? Is it for God, or for another reason?

Awe

Wow, God!

For by him all things were created,
in heaven and on earth, visible and
invisible, whether thrones or dominions
or rulers or authorities—all things were
created through him and for him.

COLOSSIANS 1:16 ESV

Sometimes we forget just how big and powerful God really is. It's easy to think of Him kind of like a superhero: a little stronger, faster, and more powerful than the rest of us. We think that way because we really can't wrap our brains around just how much stronger, faster, and more powerful God is than any superhero ever imagined.

He literally created everything on earth: every animal, every plant, every fish, every bug, every cloud in the sky, and every star at night. Everything that has ever existed or ever will exist comes from Him.

And God made you too. He made your body, mind, heart, and soul in His image. Only when you dedicate your heart to Him can you find peace, joy, and contentment. The more time you spend in God's Word and learning at His feet, the more you'll see just how amazing He truly is and the more you'll want to praise His name.

Through the Holy Spirit, you can talk to God. Through Jesus, you have God's forgiveness.

Your sin is forgiven because of His awesomeness. His sacrifice. His great love for you.

Wow.

WEEK 45
God's Splendor

*Ascribe to the L<small>ORD</small> the glory due his name;
worship the L<small>ORD</small> in the splendor of his holiness.*
Psalm 29:2

It can be really tough for us to understand just how big God really is. Try going outside on a clear night and looking up at the stars. The sky seems to stretch on forever, doesn't it? Well, God is bigger than the sky. He is brighter than all the stars you can see, brighter than the sun itself. David wrote Psalm 29 as a song of worship for God, which celebrates His power over all things in heaven and on earth and tries to express how big and wonderful God is. Try reading it aloud when you pray today.

Read the full psalm and list the characteristics or names of God that mean the most to you.

Write your own worship prayer for God here.

Mighty Things

And Mary said:

*"My soul glorifies the Lord
and my spirit rejoices in God my Savior,
for he has been mindful
of the humble state of his servant.
From now on all generations will call me blessed,
for the Mighty One has done great things for me—
holy is his name."*

Luke 1:46-49

When Mary learned she would be the mother of Jesus, she was filled with wonder and gratitude. She could have been afraid or nervous or felt like it was too much. Instead, she prayed a worship prayer to God, reflecting her joyful heart.

What about Mary's response is most surprising to you?

Make a list of the things, small or great, the Lord
has done for you recently.

WEEK 47

In God's Care

Come, let us bow down in worship,
let us kneel before the LORD our Maker;
for he is our God
and we are the people of his pasture,
the flock under his care.

Psalm 95:6-7

This psalm is filled with the joy that comes from belonging to God. How wonderful is it to be able to rest knowing we are under His care? The next time you feel scared or unsure, take a moment to remember that the same God who made *everything* is looking after you and loving you.

What image do the psalm's words create in your mind? Describe or draw it.

God is watching over you. When has knowing that helped you?

Head and Heart

Yet a time is coming and has now come when the true worshipers will worship the Father in the Spirit and in truth, for they are the kind of worshipers the Father seeks. God is spirit, and his worshipers must worship in the Spirit and in truth."

John 4:23-24

God doesn't want going-through-the-motions prayers. He wants true worshipers. He wants you to pray to Him and praise Him with everything you have: mind, body, heart, and soul.

Are you already a true worshiper of God? Why or why not?

_____

_____

_____

_____

_____

What do you think it means to worship God with your body, mind, heart, and soul?

Praise Him Anyway

Is anyone among you in trouble? Let them pray.
Is anyone happy? Let them sing songs of praise.

James 5:13

God loves to help us with our problems and support us when we need Him most. But He also wants to be beside us when life is good. He wants to laugh at our jokes, share in our happiness, and rest with us when we are at peace. So today, pray when you are happy and thank God for everything He's given you that brings you such joy.

Do you pray more when you are happy or when you are upset?

_____

_____

_____

_____

_____

Make a list of ten things that about God that bring you joy.

1. ....

2. ....

3. ....

4. ....

5. ....

6. ....

7. ....

8. ....

9. ....

10. ....

Come See

Come and see what God has done,
his awesome deeds for mankind!

Psalm 66:5

God blesses all of us in so many ways. His works should be shouted from the mountaintops so that others can see what He has done for you. When our hearts are filled with awe for Him, it's almost impossible not to tell everyone how good He is!

Have you told people about the good things God has done for you? Make a list here of things you can share with others.

Make a plan to share what God has done in your life with a friend. Which stories will you tell? Is there a verse you want to share with them?

God's Fame

LORD, I have heard of your fame;
I stand in awe of your deeds, LORD.
Repeat them in our day,
in our time make them known;
in wrath remember mercy.

Habakkuk 3:2

Habakkuk was facing down some pretty bad stuff when he wrote this verse. He wasn't talking about God's fame for being loving or kind. He was talking about God's fame for *destroying* the wicked. But in verse 18, he prayed, "Yet I will rejoice in the LORD, I will be joyful in God my Savior." When life looks scary, you can worship God because He is on your side.

Write down two situations in your world that feel scary.

What does knowing God is on your side mean to you?

Mighty and Awesome

For the LORD your God is God of gods and Lord of lords, the great God, mighty and awesome.
Deuteronomy 10:17

There is no one and nothing like God. He is so much bigger, bolder, and far above anything else that we know, yet He created it all. He is power. He is might. He is love. He is ours.

Write out what wows you most about God here.

How can you wow others in your life by being more like Him?

Great books are even better when they're shared!

Help other readers find this one:

- Post a review at your favorite online bookseller
- Post a picture on a social media account and share why you enjoyed it
- Send a note to a friend who would also love it—or better yet, give them a copy

Thanks for reading!